Franny K. Stein

MAD SCIENTIST

THE INVISIBLE FRAN

Franny K. Stein
MAD SCIENTIST

THE INVISIBLE FRAN

JIM BENTON

SCHOLASTIC INC.
New York Toronto London Auckland Sydney
Mexico City New Delhi Hong Kong Buenos Aires

ACKNOWLEDGMENTS

Senior Editor: Kevin Lewis
Art Director: Dan Potash
Managing Editor: Dorothy Gribbin
Designer: Lucy Ruth Cummins
Production Manager: Chava Wolin
Editorial Assistant: Joanna Feliz

ISBN 0-439-69261-X

12 11 10 9 8 7 6 5 4 3   5 6 7 8 9 10/0

Printed in the U.S.A.   40

First Scholastic printing, January 2005

Book design by Lucy Ruth Cummins and Dan Potash
The text for this book is set in Captain Kidd.
The illustrations for this book are rendered in pen, ink, and watercolor.

For
Kevin Lewis
and
Julie Kane-Ritsch

CONTENTS

Franny K. Stein

MAD SCIENTIST

THE INVISIBLE FRAN

CHAPTER ONE

FRANNY'S HOUSE

The Stein family lived in the pretty pink house with lovely purple shutters down at the end of Daffodil Street. Everything about the house was bright and cheery. Everything, that is, except the upstairs bedroom with the tiny round window.

The window looked in on a bedroom, yes, but it was also a window into a laboratory: Franny's laboratory. And Franny's laboratory was spectacular.

She had all of the things that you would
expect any mad scientist to have. She had an
electron microscope. She had a nuclear-powered
brain amplifier. She had a giant, flesh-eating
koala.

And she also had a few extras, a few special things that made Franny feel that her lab was just a little bit better than average.

Franny doubted that any other mad scientist had a spider enlarger or a disease simulator.

"I'll bet no more than half of them have an eyeball-removing machine," she said, thinking how fortunate she was that she could pull her own eye out.

But even if they didn't have eyeball-
removing machines or brain amplifiers or
spider enlargers, Franny suspected that her
friends—if given the chance—would love
nothing more than to set up labs of their own
and devote themselves to the pursuit of mad
science.

It was for this very reason that her teacher's next assignment inspired Franny to help her classmates see the light.

CHAPTER TWO

HOBBY DAY

Miss Shelly stood in front of the class. "We're going to talk about hobbies. Tomorrow I'd like each of you to bring in something that represents your hobby or interest."

Surely, thought Franny, many of them don't even have hobbies or interests, and even if they do, they're probably the kinds of dull hobbies that hardly ever explode or eat the neighbor's car.

Franny raised her hand. "Miss Shelly, if somebody has a hobby that doesn't involve massive amounts of electricity or sewing wings onto things that weren't born with wings, will they still be allowed to participate?"

Miss Shelly was accustomed to this sort of question from Franny.

"Yes, Franny. Everybody will get to talk about their hobbies," Miss Shelly said.

Miss Shelly was always fair, but it seemed like a waste of time to Franny, who was absolutely certain that after a little exposure to mad science, the kids would drop their other interests like hot potatoes—hot, radioactive, poisonous potatoes.

CHAPTER THREE

BACK AT THE LAB

Back at the lab Franny thought about what her presentation would be. Fortunately Franny had an assistant to help her with things like this.

Igor was Franny's dog and lab assistant. (He wasn't a *pure* Lab. He was also part poodle, part Chihuahua, part beagle, part spaniel, part shepherd, and part some kind of weasly thing that wasn't even exactly a dog.)

Franny had told Igor about Miss Shelly's assignment, and he was doing his best to make suggestions.

He reminded her of the time she had
brought a garden gnome to life and they'd had
to stay locked in the bathroom until the police
came. Igor thought the kids would like that.

"I don't want to take in a garden gnome,"
she said.

He reminded her of the time she had increased the vacuum cleaner's power and had sucked her little brother inside out.

"Mom made me promise never to do that again," she said.

He reminded her of the time she had engineered a cannibalistic hot dog that actually ate itself.

"That *was* pretty good," Franny said. "But there's a kid in my class that always smells like hot dogs, and I don't want that thing going after him. Besides, it needs to be something that everybody can relate to."

Franny walked over and looked at the dozens of devices she had recently invented. "Like this, Igor." She picked up her toenail fungus translator. "You know, deep down inside, all kids want to communicate with toenail fungus, but they've never been able to.

"Well, with this device, they finally can."
She put it in her backpack. "All the kids will
love talking to fungus. I mean, c'mon, deep
down inside, we're all mad scientists, right?"

CHAPTER FOUR
OH NO, WE'RE NOT

Miss Shelly looked around the room. Everybody was ready to talk about his or her hobbies. She pointed at Erin.

"Erin, would you like to go first?"

Erin jumped to her feet and started a tape player. As the music began, she performed a classic foot-stomping Irish dance.

The students clapped.

Franny raised her hand.

"So, Erin, about these shoes of yours. Have you ever considered splicing in a sample of mutant kangaroo DNA? It might make you bounce around in an even more uncontrolled manner."

Erin looked at Franny for a moment. "My dancing is just fine, thank you," she said, and took her seat.

Next Miss Shelly invited Lawrence to the front of the class. He pulled an accordion from a big black case and played for a minute or two before Franny raised her hand.

"Ah. Now this is *much* better. I'm certain that you could operate the keys in different ways to increase or decrease the amount of pain we're experiencing around our ear regions. My question for you is this: Have you ever thought of making a larger version that you could attach to a satellite and use to broadcast this effect over a larger area?"

Lawrence put the instrument back in the case. "It's just an accordion, Franny," he said. "I've been playing it since I was a little kid."

Next up was Phil. Miss Shelly held a large book open for him while he pointed out the various prize stamps in his collection.

"This stamp is from England," he said. "And this one is from Japan."

Franny raised her hand. "I don't suppose you've considered altering these stamps so that they explode when people lick them, have you?"

Phil shook his head. "No."

"Or doing something like transforming the postal carrier into a—oh, I don't know—a nine-foot-tall scorpion man who spews acid from his stinger and can fly, for instance?"

Miss Shelly closed the book. "Franny, Phil prefers regular, nonexploding, nontransforming postage stamps."

"Hold on," Franny said. "Just hold on one second." She walked to the front of the class. "Do you mean to tell me that *none* of you is the least bit interested in being a mad scientist?"

CHAPTER FIVE
FRANNY TOSSES HER COOKIES

Igor sat patiently and listened to Franny.

"Not *one*," she said, dropping the toenail fungus translator on the floor. "In my whole class not one other kid has even thought about conducting an experiment! Dancing, yes! Collecting, yes! Athletics, yes! But mad science, NO!"

Franny continued her rant as she checked the progress of her various experiments. "One kid had a terrarium with a chameleon, but—get this—he doesn't do any experiments with it!"

Igor wasn't crazy about chameleons since the first time Franny's giant chameleon had tried to swallow him. But he shook his head and tried to appear as though he agreed with Franny.

"I asked Miss Shelly if I could put off doing my presentation until tomorrow. After Billy shared his hobby, which is making pretty, pretty cookies, my heart just wasn't in it. Pretty, pretty cookies. I mean, seriously, Igor, that has to be the dumbest hobby of all. Imagine doing all that measuring and mixing and waiting, just for pretty, pretty cookies. Look—he even brought some in for everyone."

Franny tossed her pretty, pretty cookies in the air and shot a sizzling death ray through them.

"These kids are so misguided, Igor. They don't know what they're missing. Their interests are absolutely useless. Maybe nobody has ever really showed them why mad science is really the *only* hobby on earth."

Franny stopped and grinned broadly. "That's it, Igor. It's up to *me* to show them where they went wrong. I can show them what they should be interested in. And I can see it's going to take more than a toenail fungus translator."

CHAPTER SIX

YOU MUST BE NUTS. AND BOLTS.

Franny consulted a book from her library called *Mechanical Fiends and Hazardous Robots for Children*. Ultimately Franny created things the way she liked them, but a quick glance at some plans always got things rolling.

She worked most of the night, and with Igor's
help she had a creation that she was certain would
bring the kids around to her way of thinking.

CHAPTER SEVEN
WIRE YOU LOOKING AT MY ROBOT THAT WAY?

Franny sat at her desk, grinning. She couldn't wait to give her presentation.

"Franny," Miss Shelly said, "would you please come up here and show the class what you've brought in?"

Franny walked confidently to the front of the class. She knew that the kids would take one look at the robot and abandon their ridiculous hobbies.

She removed the sheet that had been draped over her creation. The kids gasped.

It was a robot. A few lights pulsed slowly on its chest, and they could hear a soft hum coming from inside it. Its tiny square eyes seemed to blink.

"Why does it have two heads?" one boy asked.

"Two heads are better than one," Franny said. "When it's complete, those two heads will make it *twice* as smart as the next smartest robot. Twice as useful, twice as complicated." Franny held up the robot's blueprints for the kids to see.

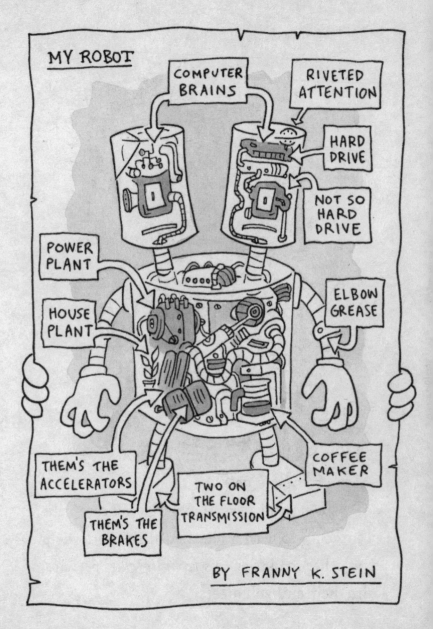

Miss Shelly said, "Franny, did you say that it wasn't complete yet?"

"That's right, Miss Shelly. It's *not* complete. I'm going to need other mad scientists to help me, other mad scientists *from the class*, perhaps. Are there any volunteers?"

Billy raised his hand.

Franny was smug. *The first of many volunteers,* she thought. "Yes," she said. "You'd like to help?"

"I would," Billy said. "*After* you finish it, I mean. Then I can teach it to bake pretty, pretty cookies."

CHAPTER EIGHT
IN THE GIZZARD OF THE LIZARD

Igor just hated to see Franny depressed. He did his best to cheer her up. He juggled spiders. He dressed up like her mom. He even thought about letting the giant chameleon swallow him a little bit, since that always made Franny laugh.

All Franny could talk about was her friends at school. "No volunteers, Igor. They all want to stick with their pointless little hobbies. They don't get it. They don't get it at all.

"They don't understand the thrill of an idea popping into your head out of nowhere, and then diving right in and making your idea just happen.

"If only they could experience that," Franny said.

Just then the giant chameleon appeared, as if out of nowhere, grabbed Igor, and swallowed him.

Even though she was depressed, Franny laughed a little and shook the chameleon until Igor fell out of its mouth. It's hard not to laugh when a reptile eats your best friend.

"You have to be more careful, Igor," Franny said.

Igor hid behind Franny.

"You know the giant chameleon can camouflage himself. It's practically like he's invisible."

Franny's eyes narrowed and a familiar grin stretched across her big, round face. "Invisible," said Franny, and she nodded slowly. "That's it. Invisible."

CHAPTER NINE

LET ME MAKE MYSELF CLEAR

The next morning Franny combined cellophane molecules with chameleon DNA and some disappearing ink. She ran the formula through an Antiscope, which is like a microscope, but it's designed to make things harder to see. She poured the formula into a very, very clean glass.

She gulped it down and ran to the mirror to see if it worked.

She liked what she saw. Or, rather, she liked
what she didn't see, which was herself.

The formula had worked. She was invisible,
and it was time for school.

CHILDREN SHOULD BE HEARD AND NOT SEEN

Invisible at school. The temptations are hard to resist, especially for one with a mind as inquisitive as Franny's.

She had a quick peek in the school's cafeteria kitchen.

She zipped in and had a look in the principal's
office.

She stopped in briefly to find out exactly what the teachers were doing in the teachers' lounge.

She found all of the locations fascinating,
but she had to get on to the next phase in her
plan: to get the kids to devote themselves to
mad science in a way that Franny knew she
should force them to want to.

Franny strolled into her class completely unseen. She walked up to Erin—who was reading—and whispered in her ear: "I think I'd like to have a look at Franny's robot again."

Erin set down her book and looked around, confused. "I-I guess I'd like to have a look at Franny's robot," she said, believing that she had thought what Franny had whispered. She walked over to the mechanical creature and began looking it over.

Next Franny did the same thing to Lawrence and Phil, and they, also believing the thoughts were their own, walked over and joined Erin.

Franny whispered to Phil, "It would be great if this robot had a huge, crushing hand, don't you think?" And Phil repeated exactly what Franny had said. Franny moved Erin's and Lawrence's heads to make it look like they were nodding yes.

All afternoon Franny kept giving them one idea after another. She also checked and double-checked that the adjustments they were making were correct. Erin, Lawrence, and Phil got more and more excited as they worked on the robot, believing that they were the ones responsible.

By the end of the day Franny was exhausted but happy. She had made a lot of progress on the robot, and her friends thought that they had contributed.

Back at home Franny took the invisibility antidote and told Igor all about the experiment. "It was a little bit funny, Igor. They really thought they were working on the robot. Of course they're not qualified to do anything that complicated yet," she said. "I'm not sure that Phil could even put batteries in a flash-light.

"But they had fun, and it boosted their confidence, and maybe now they'll stop wasting time on those ridiculous diversions."

Franny climbed into bed and drifted off to dream her mad science dreams, unaware that back at school something quite mad, but quite unscientific, was about to happen.

CHAPTER ELEVEN

SNEAKING OUT TO JOIN THE CIRCUITS

Erin, Lawrence, and Phil crept quietly into the school. They were wearing outfits unlike any they had worn before. They were dressed like mad scientists.

They had tools and notes and devices that
no real scientist would use to finish a partially
built robot.

And yet that is exactly what they intended
to do.

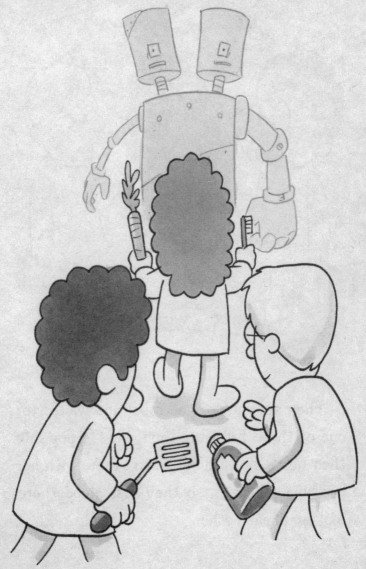

They surrounded the robot and waited for one of those brilliant "thoughts" to pop into their heads. But Franny wasn't there with her invisible whispers, so they just stood there, looking at each other.

After a while Phil became impatient and decided to pretend to have a brilliant thought. "It should be able to squirt ketchup from its nozzle right here," he said. The other two nodded.

"It needs to be able to extend this, like so," Erin said, also faking an idea.

"And I have a few changes I think we should make to its brain," said Lawrence, who sometimes had trouble changing his pants, much less a robot's brain.

"We are totally mad scientists now," Erin said as she pulled carelessly at wires in the robot's chest.

"There's nothing to it," Lawrence said, recklessly joining circuits inside one of the robot's brains.

"And Franny hardly did any of the work on this robot. It's really more our robot than hers," Phil added, and the robot beeped.

CHAPTER TWELVE
THE NEW ROBOT IS A SMASH HIT

Franny walked happily into her classroom. She was thinking about maybe rescuing more kids from stupid hobbies.

She was surprised, as anyone might be, to find that most of her classroom had been smashed to smithereens. (Note: For anybody doing the conversion, there are ten smithers in an ounce, and ten smithereens in a smither.)

Erin climbed from underneath a smoldering chunk of desk. "Thank goodness," she said. "Another mad scientist to help us."

Franny raised one eyebrow. "'Another' mad scientist? What do you mean by 'another'? You're not a mad scientist."

Lawrence and Phil climbed out from their hiding places. "Sure we are," Phil said. "You should have seen us yesterday."

"That's right," Lawrence added. "And we finished the robot last night."

"You finished it?" Franny shouted. "You're not qualified to do that. What made you think you could create and activate something that complex and dangerous?"

The three of them just looked down at their feet.

Then it suddenly occurred to Franny. *She* was what made them think that.

"I have a very bad feeling about this," Franny said.

CHAPTER THIRTEEN

FOOLS + TOOLS = BUSTED-UP SCHOOLS

Franny scribbled some computations on the robot's blueprint. She reviewed the notes that Erin, Lawrence, and Phil had given her, and tried to include in her calculations what they could remember about the extra work they had done during the night.

They could hear the robot starting on a new rampage somewhere else in the school.

Franny finished her computations. "Egad," she gasped.

"What? What is it?" Lawrence squeaked.

"I designed the robot with two heads because, as you know, two heads would make it twice as smart as a regular robot."

Phil tried to look like he understood.

"But you guys, well, you don't know the first thing about robots, or electronics, or science, or machines, or maybe anything."

Erin scowled a bit, but this was no time to argue.

"You see, because you know nothing, you actually made this robot twice as *stupid* as a regular robot."

"So will that make it easier to stop?" Lawrence asked hopefully.

"Hand me my backpack," Franny said sternly.

CHAPTER FOURTEEN

STUPIDER AND STUPIDER

Franny took another dose of her invisibility formula. "It can't smash what it can't see," she said, trying her best to sound optimistic. And she faded from their sight.

Most monstrous fiends, even though they are often horribly destructive, have a plan. Either they want something, they hate something, or they're just trying to escape capture. So it's easy for a scientific mind to figure them out and stop them.

This thing is different, Franny thought. *This robot is pure stupidness. It has two whole heads full of stupid. Pure stupidness does things for no good reason.*

What would a pure-stupid creature do in a school? Franny thought.

THE PRINSIPUL HAS A RUBBER Butt

Franny ran past a door on which the robot had left some graffiti. It was badly spelled, badly drawn, and not at all clever. "In addition," Franny said, "it's probably inaccurate. If the principal really *did* have a rubber butt, surely by now they would have flown her to consult with a medical expert in Switzerland."

Franny ran past gigantic spit wads that the robot had left dangling from the ceiling and dripping down the walls.

"Spit wads," she said. "Can you imagine
wasting perfectly good spit this way? Spit, like
most secretions, is hours of fun for a child with
a microscope. Only an idiot would squander it
this way."

Spitty robot footprints led right up to the
library door, and Franny actually felt an
unfamiliar wave of fear wash over her.

"Not the books," she said.

CHAPTER FIFTEEN
FRANNY KETCHES UP TO THE ROBOT

Franny slid quietly into the library. She knew the robot was in there somewhere.

She could have overlooked the graffiti. Franny had made inaccurate speculations about butts before. Butts are an imprecise science; errors occur.

And she might even have been able to find some merit in giant spit wads. She had to admit that they had a sort of charm to them, like a fresh snowfall—a fresh snowfall that smelled like the inside of somebody's mouth.

But Franny *loved* books. She loved everything about them. Most of what Franny knew she had learned from books. A creature this stupid could be in the library for only one reason: to destroy books. And an act that stupid was not going to be tolerated.

She moved silently and cautiously.

And then she heard it: the sad, sick sound of a page slowly being torn from a book. She crept through the aisles.

She rounded a corner and saw the robot there, happily destroying books. It was clear to Franny that this mechanical imbecile would not stop until it had destroyed all of them.

As she studied the horrible creation, she suddenly felt confident that defeating this robot was going to be quite easy. In fact, she felt very confident.

Evidently Erin, Lawrence, and Phil had installed an off switch right in the middle of the robot's chest.

All Franny had to do was quietly walk up to it, totally unseen, and flip the switch.

"Actually, that was pretty clever of them," Franny whispered, "to install an off switch in such a convenient location."

And if Franny had thought it through for just a split second longer, she would have realized that Erin, Phil, and Lawrence were not qualified to come up with something as clever as a chest-mounted off switch that would actually work.

But she hadn't thought it through, and she
did flip the switch, which was not wired to turn
off the robot, of course, but *was* wired to squirt
a huge gush of ketchup from its newly
installed ketchup nozzle.

The books! Franny leapt through the air and dove in front of a shelf full of books, heroically protecting them from the sloppy condiment onslaught but at the same time taking the full impact of the ketchup herself, thus rendering herself totally visible to the robot.

CHAPTER SIXTEEN

HERE, LET ME GIVE YOU A HAND

Crash! The robot smashed Franny with its giant hand.

Erin, Lawrence, and Phil heard it and rushed into the library.

"We'll save you, Franny!" they shouted. They folded their arms just like they had seen Franny do. "It's mad science time," they said.

The robot swung at Franny again. She tried to dodge, but it caught her hard. *SMASH!*

"Uh, got some mad science coming right up," the kids said, looking at each other helplessly. The robot's hand came down with another mighty crash. *BASH!* Franny didn't think she could last much longer.

Then Franny did what she did best. She *thought*, and she thought fast.

"Maybe, maybe a mad scientist is exactly what we *don't* need," she said. *SMASH!* She took another powerful slam from the robot's hand.

She looked over at her friends, and then it suddenly came to her. Franny knew exactly what they needed.

"What we need is a philatelist!" she yelled.

"A what?" Erin shouted back.

"A philatelist is a stamp collector," Phil said. "Like me."

"Phil!" Franny yelled. "The eyes!"

Phil knew exactly what Franny meant. A pair of stamps would cover the robot's little square eyes perfectly. Phil pulled out a pair of stamps from his pocket and with a lick and a slap, had them across the robot's eyes.

Now blinded, the robot missed Franny
entirely. And its metal hands were too big and
clumsy to remove the stamps.

"Now what we need is an accordionist!" Franny shouted, and Lawrence leapt into action. Grabbing one of the robot's heads in his right hand and the other head in his left, Lawrence began flexing his powerful deltoid and trapezius muscles, built up by years of music lessons.

The robot reeled and fell under Lawrence's mighty accordionist blows.

CLANG
CLANG
CLANG

"Now what we need is . . . ," Franny began, but Erin was already one step ahead of her.

"An Irish dancer," Erin said, and began hammering out a merciless hail of rhythmic stomps on the fallen robot, sending gears and wires in all directions.

When the dust finally settled, the four of them stood there looking at the pile of broken, flattened, robot parts.

It was over. They had won. They had been saved by philately, accordionism, and Gaelic choreography.

CHAPTER SEVENTEEN

NOW YOU'RE COOKING

Later, back at the lab, Franny and Igor were completing Franny's newest project. She had explained what had happened that day, and Igor wondered if Franny knew just how extremely lucky she was to have friends that were not mad scientists.

Franny put down her welding torch. "At last, it's complete," she said.

"Igor," Franny said, handing him a piece of paper, "run downstairs and get these items. Quickly; I'll need them for this next experiment."

Igor began to read the list as he ran: *Sugar, flour, milk*...

Franny picked up the phone and paused to look at her newest creation.

She dialed the phone. "Billy?" she said.

Igor walked in with the ingredients, bowls, and cookie sheets Franny had requested.

"How would you like to come up to the lab and, um, share some of your techniques with me?" Igor heard Franny say.

Erin's dance had stamped the robot into nice, flat pieces that Franny had spent a long time cutting and welding into what was probably the best pastry oven in the world.

Franny K. Stein, mad scientist, was going to bake pretty, pretty cookies.

"He'll be right over," Franny beamed, and Igor smiled.